From the
Library of:

ALSO BY JUDITH VIORST

LULU

Is Getting a Sister

(Who WANTS Her? Who NEEDS Her?)

JUDITH VIORST

illustrated by KEVIN CORNELL

A Caitlyn Dlouhy Book

Atheneum Books for Young Readers

NEW YORK • LONDON • TORONTO • SYDNEY • NEW DELHI

ATHENEUM BOOKS FOR YOUNG READERS

An imprint of Simon & Schuster Children's Publishing Division

1230 Avenue of the Americas, New York, New York 10020

This book is a work of fiction. Any references to historical events, real people, or real places are used fictitiously. Other names, characters, places, and events are products of the author's imagination, and any resemblance to actual events or places or persons, living or dead, is entirely coincidental.

ATHENEUM BOOKS FOR YOUNG READERS is a registered trademark of Simon & Schuster, Inc. Atheneum logo is a trademark of Simon & Schuster, Inc.

For information about special discounts for bulk purchases, please contact Simon & Schuster Special Sales at 1-866-506-1949 or business@simonandschuster.com.

The Simon & Schuster Speakers Bureau can bring authors to your live event. For more information or to book an event, contact the Simon & Schuster Speakers Bureau at 1-866-248-3049 or visit our website at www.simonspeakers.com.

Also available in an Atheneum Books for Young Readers hardcover edition

Book design by Ann Bobco

The text for this book was set in Officina Sands.

The illustrations for this book were rendered in graphite and watercolor on paper and then digitally manipulated.

Manufactured in the United States of America

0719 MTN

First Atheneum Books for Young Readers paperback edition September 2019

10 9 8 7 6 5 4 3 2 1

The Library of Congress has cataloged the hardcover edition as follows:

Names: Viorst, Judith, author.

Title: Lulu is getting a sister (Who wants her? Who needs her?) / Judith Viorst.

Description: First edition. | New York : Simon & Schuster, [2018] | "A Caitlyn Dlouhy book." | Summary: "Lulu is sent to Camp Sisterhood to learn how to be a big sister, but she makes it her mission to be the worst sister in training in camp history"—Provided by publisher.

Identifiers: LCCN 2016034463 | ISBN 9781481471909 (hardcover) | ISBN 9781481471916 (pbk) ISBN 9781481471923 (ebook)

Subjects: | CYAC: Sisters—Fiction. | Camps—Fiction.

Classification: LCC PZ7.V816 Luo 2018 | DDC [Fic]—dc23

LC record available at https://lccn.loc.gov/2016034463

This story is dedicated, with love, to
Michelle Halpern Viorst.
—J. V.

For Kim, who holds my hand
—K. C.

Lulu *must have forgotten that* TANTRUM *because . . .*

She's down on the floor, and *she's kicking* her heels, and she's waving her arms around, and she's also screeching her lightbulbs-bursting screech. And her mom and her dad are nervously holding on to each other because they never know what to do when their darling Lulu, their precious Lulu, is *being . . .* D I F F I C U L T .

The reason she's being difficult— or what some of us call a really

she's too old to be having a

SHE'S HAVING ONE.

big pain in the butt—is that she
has just been told that in a few
months she will be getting A BABY
SISTER!!!!!!!!!

No, not a baby*sitter*—that was the
last book. I *said* a baby SISTER—
and that's what I meant.

Now Lulu, you won't be surprised to hear, has zero interest in having a baby sister. She has always, *always* liked being an only child. And don't bother asking her WON'T IT BE NICE TO HAVE A PAL TO HANG WITH?, for she's going to say she has plenty of pals to hang with: like Mr. B, a charming brontosaurus. Like Fleischman, a helpful though deeply annoying boy. And even like the mysteriouso Sonia Sofia Solinsky, whose secrets

Lulu has sworn to never reveal.

However, what Lulu *will reveal* is how firmly, fiercely, ferociously she doesn't want to have a baby sister. So if you're a little sister (or brother) you probably won't appreciate this book. But if you're an older sister (or brother) you'll probably understand why Lulu, getting up from the floor, is telling her mom and her dad, "YOU'VE RUINED MY LIFE!"

chapter one

It made no sense to Lulu that her mom and her dad were so happy about this baby. Why in the world would they need another child? And why would they want a girl, when they've already GOT a girl, namely Lulu, who totally had this girl-in-the-family thing covered?

And wasn't her mom always hugging her and saying, in the mushiest tone of voice, "You are the greatest treasure of our life"?

And wasn't her dad always hugging her and saying, with this little sob in his voice, "Nothing on earth brings your mother and me more joy"?

Not to mention all those times her mom and her dad had told her, "Our hearts are filled to the brim with love for you."

So how come—if their hearts were filled to the brim—there was room left in their hearts for another kid?

Lulu didn't bother asking that question. Instead, arms folded across her chest, and a glittery glare in her eyes, she icily said to her mom and her dad, "Maybe I won't be talking to you anymore. Maybe I'll go into my room and never come out. Maybe I'll hold my breath and keep on holding and holding and holding it till I turn blue. Or maybe I'll find a new mom and dad who'll think that I'm so special that they'd never want or need another kid."

"WE think you're special!" said Lulu's mom.

"Very!" said Lulu's dad.

"Hah!" said Lulu. "Hah!" Then she stomped away.

chapter two

Lulu stomped into the kitchen, where she crouched—knees to chin—underneath the table, an excellent place to brood and sulk and be mad. Her parents, tiptoeing timidly, followed her as far as the kitchen door.

"We thought you might not be completely thrilled with this news," said Lulu's mom, "so we made a plan."

"To help you," her dad said, "get ready for a sister."

"Ready? There's no ready!" said Lulu, going on to declare, "I don't and will never want to *have* a sister. I'm not and will never want to *be* a sister." She paused for a moment, then asked with sudden suspicion, "You said you had a plan. What kind of plan?"

There was silence.

"Tell me about this plan!" said Lulu.

More silence.

After which Lulu's mom and her dad, edging into the kitchen, started frantically whispering to each other. Whisper. Pause. Whisper. Pause. Whisper. Pause. Whisper. And then . . .

"Rather than tell you about it . . . ,"
began Lulu's mom.

". . . we think you should read about it,"
Lulu's dad finished.

"I don't like how this is sounding," Lulu
said.

And she liked it even less when her
dad, reaching into his pocket and then
down under the table, handed her a
colorful brochure, a brochure whose cover
proclaimed, in great
big letters:

chapter three

While her mom and her dad waited anxiously, Lulu started reading, growing grouchier with every word.

CAMP SISTERHOOD is designed to provide a happy sister experience for girls accustomed to being an only child. As sisters-in-training (SITs), they'll work and play and share with younger children, having so much fun with their temporary little "sisters" or little "brothers" that they'll soon want permanent siblings of their own.

(In case you didn't know that "siblings" means brothers or sisters or both, now you do. And though it's kind of a clunky word, I'm going to have to use it more than I like.)

The brochure that Lulu was reading explained that Camp Sisterhood had been specially created for older girls without any brothers or sisters, girls who had always believed they would be the only child in the family, girls who after many blissful years of only-ness were going to have to share life with another kid. The

brochure showed many pictures of sisters-in-training and younger "siblings" oh-so-happily sharing life with each other. None of these pictures made Lulu the slightest bit happy.

She climbed out from under the kitchen table and scowled—scowled long and hard—at her mom and her dad. "Here's what I have to say to your plan: I'm not going."

"But dearest darling, it's just for two weeks," said her mom.

"We've already signed you up for it," said her dad.

"Then UNsign me up. You can't make me go!" said Lulu very loudly.

To which her mom replied, while her dad kept nodding his head in agreement, "But maybe we can make you *want* to go."

Make her *want* to go? What in the world was *that* supposed to mean? Were Lulu's mom and dad warning her that if she didn't go, they'd take away her cell phone and her computer? Give her a lot of time-outs, and no more desserts? Were they getting all strict and all stern, for surely the first time ever, letting her know that they'd make her go by making her real sorry if she didn't? And would our Lulu, scared they might actually mean it, decide that she'd better *want* to go to Camp Sisterhood?

Don't be ridiculous!

Lulu's mom and her dad would never try to make Lulu do anything by *scaring* her. They were more scared of Lulu than she was of them. They only would try, as they always had tried, and as they're about to try now, to get her to do what they wanted her to by *bribing* her. By giving her, and letting her do, good stuff. Lots of good stuff. So much good stuff that she'd *want* to change her mind. But getting Lulu to change her mind, as a ton of tantrums has taught them, would not be easy.

"So here's what we've been thinking," said Lulu's mom. "We've been thinking that after you spend two weeks at Camp Sisterhood, we're going to let you redecorate your room."

Lulu, wearing a bored that's-supposed-to-*thrill*-me? look on her face, just shrugged her shoulders.

"And double your allowance," said her dad.

Lulu, sighing a deep that-really-doesn't-impress-me sigh, once again shrugged her shoulders.

"You'll also be allowed," said her mom, "to stay up as late as you want—during the week as well as on the weekends."

Lulu was beginning to look interested.

"And also, your grandma Gertie, who was saving this treat until you were much, much older, has agreed," said her mom, "to take you up for a ride in a hot-air balloon as soon as you are finished at Camp Sisterhood."

"I want that balloon ride *before* I go to Camp Sisterhood," said Lulu. "The rest of the stuff can wait till I come back."

WHOA! STOP! HOLD IT RIGHT THERE! DO YOU UNDERSTAND WHAT JUST HAPPENED? LULU, DIFFICULT LULU, STUBBORN LULU, IMPOSSIBLE LULU HAS CHANGED. HER. MIND!

Well, sort of.

Lulu has figured out that her mom and her dad must have had a lot of conversations, not only with the folks up there at Camp Sisterhood, but also with Grandma Gertie and "Call me Debbie." That was the lady at Lulu's school who, if a student seemed what she called "a bit troubled," would invite the student's parents to come in for what she called "a friendly chat." That was the lady who always came up with another silly suggestion for how, as she put it, "Mom and Dad and their Lulu could be a more coordinated team."

(Coordinated, like everyone getting along with everyone else, and no one being a really big pain in the butt? Good luck with that!)

Surely Call-Me-Debbie must have told Lulu's mom and her dad about Camp Sisterhood. And surely Grandma Gertie must have helped them pick out all those excellent bribes. But what nobody seemed to get was that Lulu could go to Camp Sisterhood for a thousand years, and she'd still never want to have, or to be, a sister. What no one seemed to get was that Lulu could hang around with a thousand little "sisters" and still not want a permanent one of her own. She would go to this useless Camp Sisterhood and be an SIT so she could collect all the good stuff that had been promised to her. But a happy sister experience? No way.

chapter four

Let's skip past the end of Lulu's school year and the start of her summer vacation and the hot-air-balloon ride she took with her grandma Gertie. Let's get her up to Camp Sisterhood, where her tearful mom and her dad have brought and hugged and kissed and finally left her. Right now it's Sunday afternoon, and she's sitting there with the other SITs, listening to a speech by the counselor-in-chief. And this counselor-in-chief (who has turned out to be none other than Call-Me-Debbie) is telling the SITs what they'll be experiencing during their "wondrous, life-expanding" two weeks.

"Wondrous? Life-expanding?" Lulu muttered under her breath. "Yeah, right."

"No negativity, please," urged Call-Me-Debbie with a smile, hastening on to explain that there were eighty sisters-in-training at the camp, that they ranged in age from eleven to fourteen, and that they would be living together in "cozy" groups of ten in eight "homey" log cabins.

"Cozy? Homey? Log cabins? Are you kidding me?" grumped Lulu, who had already looked at her cabin and already hated it. There were drafty spaces between the logs, there were little buggy

things crawling around on the floor,
and if you needed to pee or worse in the
middle of the night, you had to leave your
cabin and go to a bathroom in the woods,
carrying a flashlight so you wouldn't
accidentally step on a snake.

Call-Me-Debbie, round as a beach ball
and smiling her shining smile, waggled
a finger at Lulu and chirped, "Think
positive." She then went on to inform
them that, across the lake from Camp
Sisterhood, you could see the almost-
exactly-the-same Camp Brotherhood,
where boys whose mothers were also
expecting babies were spending the same
two weeks being *brothers*-in-training.
"And at the end of that time," she

continued, still smiling her bright, big-toothed smile, "both of the camps will get together and celebrate—with fun and games and a yummy, delicious meal."

"Yummy? Delicious? Give me a break," said a disgusted Lulu, who'd already tasted the food and already hated it. Veggie burgers! Cucumber salad! Stewed fruit for dessert! She'd rather starve.

"Be positive! Not negative!" the ever-smiling Call-Me-Debbie told Lulu. "We're here to chase negativity away. And we'll start right now by presenting your adorable little 'brothers' and little 'sisters,' who—in your wondrous, life-expanding encounters—will make you stop wanting to be an only child."

Forty wriggling, squirming, whining five-to-eight-year-olds were then marched into Camp Sisterhood's main building.

Lulu had read in the camp brochure that this bunch of little kids, along with their (mostly) moms or (just a few) dads, would also be spending two wondrous weeks at Camp Sisterhood. Except that they would be living not in log cabins, but in cottages

with bathrooms inside and no crawly
things on the floor. These would be the
children who the sisters-in-training would
be practicing on. These would be the
children who Lulu and all the SITs would
be working with and playing with and
sharing with. Lulu, just being curious,
dug deep down into herself to see if she
felt any hint of sisterly feelings.

Nope.

chapter five

After Call-Me-Debbie had shown off and sent off the little kids, she handed out a list to each SIT, a list of Sisterly Tips that would help to assure them, she assured them, of a "wondrous, life-expanding" time at Camp Sisterhood. Lulu went back to her cabin where, before curling up with her favorite vampire book, she impatiently looked over the Sisterly Tips list.

Tip 1. Never forget that you're here to get yourself used to having a little brother or sister. Treat the boy or girl you've been assigned to as if he or she really *is* your brother or sister. Try to find things to love, no matter how hard it is to find them, about your little brother or little sister. And always try to remember there are things he or she finds hard to love about you.

What kinds of things, Lulu wondered, would a little brother or sister possibly find hard to love about *her*? She couldn't think of any. Not a one.

Tip 2. Try to choose activities that you and your younger sibling will *both* enjoy. If these involve *competing* with each other, like racing or board games, be nice and let her or him win some of the time.

This tip made no sense to Lulu, who wondered how, if she was competing, she could be nice. (Especially because it was hard enough for her to be nice when she *wasn't* competing.)

Tip 3. When your younger sibling is making a birdhouse or bookmark in arts and crafts, or figuring out a clue in a scavenger hunt, you need to be patient. Let him or her make mistakes, or take a long time, or say "I can't do this," before you gently, kindly offer to help. No rolling of eyes. No heavy sighs. And you're NEVER allowed to say, "You messed up again?" or "How dumb can you get!" or—if there are tears—"Wah! Wah! Big crybaby!"

So what exactly, Lulu wondered, ARE you supposed to say when the dumb crybaby messes up again?

Tip 4. There will be no biting, scratching, kicking, hair-pulling, foot-stomping, punching, poking, or pinching, even if your younger sibling bites or scratches or kicks you, or pulls your hair or stomps on both your feet, or gives you a punch or a poke or a pinch or whatever. Instead, you'll explain to her or to him that we at Camp Sisterhood deeply believe in nonviolence, that no one is ever permitted to hurt someone else, and that when we're mad or sad and really want to zap somebody, we use respectful, sisterly words instead.

Lulu completely agreed that we ought to use words whenever we're feeling mad or sad, but first—a zap.

Tip 5. Perhaps the hardest problem a big sister has to face is sharing with a younger sister or brother—sharing a room, a dessert, certain games, certain toys. In addition, because they can't help it, a younger brother or sister will take and mess around with stuff that is only YOURS, completely YOURS. So unless you really love sharing (which you probably don't, though it would be great if you did), you need to find a firm but pleasant way to tell your sibling, "That's YOURS. This is MINE." To which we suggest you sweetly add, "And if you want to use mine, you must ask my permission," rather than a not-so-sweet, "And keep your grubby hands off my stuff—or else."

Lulu had no intention of letting anyone's grubby hands get anywhere *near* her stuff.

After she'd finished reading, Lulu put down the Sisterly Tips and gave some serious thought to tip number five. It talked about sharing stuff. But what it didn't talk about was sharing not just stuff, but your mom and your dad. Sharing your mom and your dad with another person. A person who will become your actual sibling. A sibling whose actual mom and dad are also *your* mom and dad. A sibling who will now expect to receive from *your* mom and dad as much love, time, attention, and goodies as *you* get. This was a nightmare!

There was no way Lulu was sharing
her mom or her dad or even her goldfish
with anyone. So if all these nicey-nice
tips were supposed to make her actually
happy to have a sister, THIS DEFINITELY
WAS *NOT* GOING TO HAPPEN. There'd be
no finding things to love. Or enjoying. Or
kindly and gently. There'd be no patiently
waiting. No offers of help. In fact, if they
were giving a prize for the Worst SIT in
the History of Camp Sisterhood, Lulu was
determined to do her utterly, totally,
Lulu-est best to win it.

chapter six

The morning after Lulu arrived, having passed an uncomfortable night talking herself out of needing to go to the bathroom, the sisters-in-training training began with a bang. Each SIT was assigned her own little "sister" or "brother"—to be with four hours a day, six days a week, on either a morning or an afternoon shift.

(And just in case you're wondering, yes, I've done the arithmetic right. It's forty kids for eighty SITs. Because, if you're paying attention, you'll see that each of the sisters-in-training gets a kid for only HALF a day.)

(And regarding Lulu's question that, if you truly couldn't stand the kid you were given, could you exchange him or her for somebody else, the answer is no.)

(And also, in case you're wondering, the sisters-in-training never practice on babies, or on "brothers" or "sisters" under five. The reason for this, which you'll need to ask your mom or your dad to explain, has to do with something called insurance.)

(And no once again to Lulu, who once again is asking the question, if you truly *hated* the kid, could you trade her in. Like the baby your mom will be bringing home, your approval doesn't matter—you and the kid are together for the duration.)

During this duration, they were told, each SIT and her kid will engage in many kinds of outdoor and indoor activities, in the course of which the SITs will learn to treat their little brothers and sisters with niceness and kindness and sweetness and sibling love.

The SITs also were warned, however, that there were bound to be a few problems along the way and to be prepared for some "disappointing" behavior. Because even the dearest and sweetest of children will sometimes do what they shouldn't and get on your nerves. (Hey, what a shock!) And even the nicest of SITs will sometimes lose their patience and get annoyed. (Who would have thought!) But there's nothing you need to worry about, the SITs were assured, since a parent would always be lurking in the background, keeping his or her eye on things but never interfering— unless something *really* bad was about to occur.

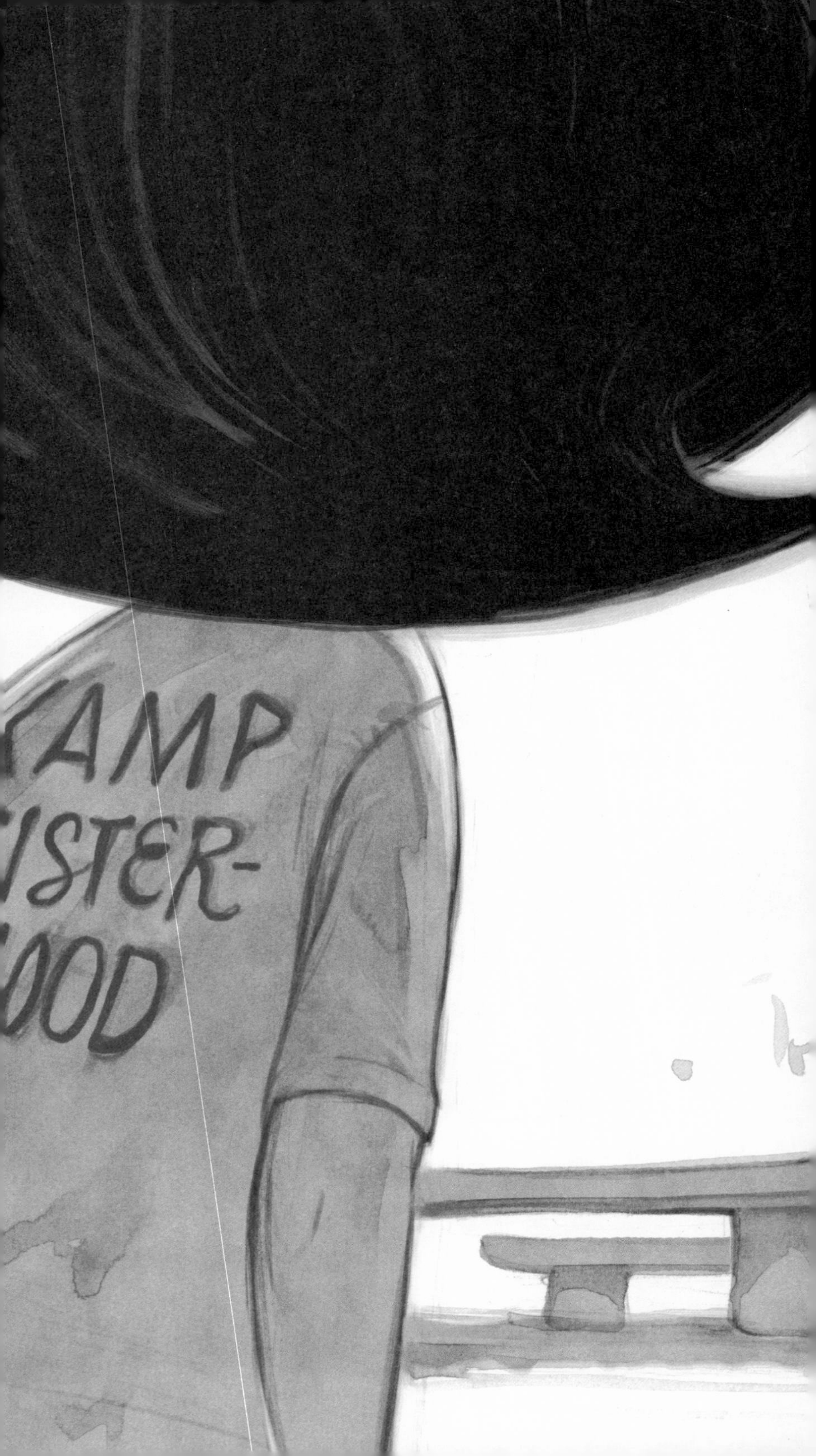
AMP
ISTER-
OOD

"So who decides?" asked Lulu, before she went off with the kid she'd been given. "Who decides when something's about to get bad?"

"I guess we'll find out," the kid answered, even though Lulu wasn't asking her. "But now I want to tell you all about ME."

chapter seven

Lulu, who was NOT in the mood for friendly conversation, grabbed the kid's hand and headed for the door. But there wasn't a second of silence because this pint-size, blue-eyed, button-nosed, frizzy-haired talking machine started talk-talk-talking and never shut up.

"So hello, I'm Mitzi, I'm eight—well, practically eight—and I'm a twin, and my birthday, both our birthdays, is August ninth, and my favorite color is silver, and my favorite song is 'Somewhere Over the Rainbow,' and my favorite movie is—I still can't decide—and I love doing cartwheels and jumping rope and lots of other fun things, like," and without even taking a breath, she raced through a very long list of those other fun things, pausing finally to ask an impatient, finger-and-foot-tapping Lulu, "But there's one thing I'm super-good at—wanna guess what it is?"

"Just *tell* me already," said Lulu. "Let's get this over with."

"Scrabble," said Mitzi. "Scrabble. I can play that game better than practically anyone else. No matter who I am playing against, even boys and girls who are older than *you*, I usually win."

(Scrabble. You know about Scrabble, right? But just in case you don't, I'm going to try to explain it to you—fast.

Each player starts with seven small tiles, each of which has its own letter. These letters are used to make words on the Scrabble board. Some of the letters will get you high points, and so will some of the words, if they're placed on spaces that double or triple your score. So if you're clever about where you're placing your words, and if you know lots of weird words using x, q, and z, you'll be the player who gets the most points, you'll be the highest scorer, you'll be the winner of the Scrabble game.)

Lulu, you won't be surprised to hear, wins most of her Scrabble games. She beats her dad and her mom and her grandma Gertie. She expects to win whenever she plays, which is why she is feeling annoyed by what this not-yet-eight-year-old Mitzi is saying. In fact

she is feeling EXTREMELY ANNOYED that
this little kid seems to believe that if she
played Scrabble with Lulu, she—Mitzi!—
would win.

"So you're super-good?" growled Lulu,
pulling Mitzi into Camp Sisterhood's
indoor-games cabin. "We'll see about
that. Sit down—we're playing Scrabble."

Less than an hour later, Mitzi had beaten
Lulu—badly—by using outrageous words
like "oxo" and "zarf," and getting extra
points by using all seven of her letters
to make another dumb word that no
one had heard of.

(If you're wondering what that
word was, I'm happy to tell you—it's
"cacique," a kind of a bird. If you're
wondering what the score was,
I've decided not to tell you—it's too
embarrassing.)

Mitzi wasn't worried about embarrassing.

She jumped up out of her chair and twirled around in a victory dance and then she shouted, maybe a hundred times, "I won! I won! I won! I won! I won!" After which she cheerfully said to a very uncheerful Lulu, "And what do you have to say about *that*, older sister?"

Lulu narrowed her eyes and not-too-nicely answered Mitzi. "I've got two things to say to you," she said. "One,

I'd rather have a cavity,
A bellyache, a blister,
A splinter, or mosquito bites
Than be your older sister,

so you can just stop calling me that right now. And two, sit down. We're playing another game."

This time the Scrabble game went a whole lot faster. It ended with Mitzi having the higher score. And after she danced her victory dance and did her "I wons" once more, Lulu, red in the face, said, "We're playing again."

They played again. And yet again Mitzi beat Lulu. And yet again Mitzi danced her dance and "I won-ed."

As Lulu was clearing the tiles from the board so they could start the next game, Mitzi objected. "We're not supposed to be *inside* all morning," she said. "We also need to be *outside*, going swimming and other fun things, but all we've done for almost four hours is Scrabble. I really want to go swimming before they ring the bell for lunch. And besides, it's boring— beating you all the time."

(Uh-oh, Mitzi has just gone too far. Way too far. For along with all that shouting and dancing whenever she beat Lulu, she now was *nyah-nyah-nyah*ing, rubbing it in. Nobody dares to treat Lulu that way unless—like Mitzi—they simply don't know what they're doing or they foolishly think that it might be amusing to see how Lulu gets ready to throw a tantrum. It is NOT amusing.)

Lulu's face, which was already red, became redder. Her hands clenched into fists. Her eyes kind of popped. And although steam actually didn't (and actually couldn't) come out of her ears, anyone looking at Lulu might think that it had. Which is why a mother (one of those parents—remember?—who lurked in the background) decided that something bad was about to occur. And why, just as Lulu was getting ready to throw herself down on the floor and do her heel-kicking, arm-waving, screeching-until-all-the-lightbulbs-burst tantrum-y stuff, this mother dashed out from the background and poured a bucket of water on Lulu's head.

chapter eight

Twenty minutes later, after Lulu had changed into dry clothes, Lulu and Mitzi were sitting in the office of a smiling Call-Me-Debbie.

The mom who had poured the water on Lulu's head had left the room, after explaining why she'd done what she'd done—"It was like there was *steam* coming out of her ears." And now the girls were taking turns insisting that what had happened had absolutely been the other girl's fault.

"Feelings were hurt. Tempers were lost. And lessons need to be learned," said Call-Me-Debbie, giving each girl an encouraging pat on the hand and (I need to stop saying this) still smiling. "So . . . what are these lessons?"

"You shouldn't be a sore loser, " said Mitzi.

"You shouldn't be a rude winner," Lulu replied.

"That's excellent, girls. Just listen
to each other. And also," said Call-Me-
Debbie, "when you meet tomorrow
morning, try doing a little less inside, a
little more outside."

She paused for a moment, perhaps to
make sure they were listening to *her*,
and then she repeated warningly, "Don't
forget—less inside and more outside. Or
else it's going to go on your permanent
record."

Lulu had no idea what "go on your permanent record" meant (and neither do I) but she knew that she didn't like the way it sounded. So when she and her sibling met on Tuesday morning, she announced that they'd skip the games cabin and head directly down to the lake for a swim.

When they reached the water's edge, Lulu said, "Let's race. And just to make it fair," (and because she figured she'd win by a mile) "I'll give you a head start by counting slowly to ten before I jump in."

By the time Lulu finished counting, however, the race was already over and she had lost. Lost to this pint-size not-yet-eight-year-old. "Next time I'm only counting to five," she announced, but it didn't help—she lost to this pint-size, frizzy-haired not-yet-eight-year-old. And even when Lulu said, "You're not getting any more head starts," she was beaten a third, a fourth, and then a fifth time— beaten five times in a row by this pint-size, frizzy-haired, button-nosed not-yet-eight-year-old!

Who did just a little victory dance and only a few "I wons," then stroked Lulu's arm with pity in her eyes. "Poor Lulu," she said. "But you shouldn't feel bad. Please do not feel bad. You tried so hard. You did the best you could."

"I don't need YOU feeling sorry for ME!" said Lulu, who was absolutely outraged that she was being treated so—what's the right word?—so . . . (I think we should go with "condescendingly," which is when a person believes she's so much better and so much greater than somebody else that

she acts all gooey and kind to the poor little thing) . . . condescendingly.

"I'm only feeling sorry for you because there's no way you could beat me," she replied. "I've been on a swim team ever since I was three. But," (and there she goes again, stroking Lulu's arm) "you swam very well. You did some excellent kicking. Good job."

Lulu did NOT want to hear "good job" from some pint-size, frizzy-haired, button-nosed, blue-eyed, incredibly irritating not-yet-eight-year-old. "Stop talking, Mitzi," she shouted, "and listen to me!"

"Wait, first listen to *me*. There's something important I've got to tell you," the girl insisted.

"Like more things," Lulu growled, "you do better than me?"

"No, it's about a little trick that just got played on you." She cleared her throat and said softly, "I'm Fritzi, not Mitzi."

"Say that again?" asked Lulu, who couldn't believe what she'd just heard.

"I'm Fritzi, Mitzi's twin, and no one can ever tell us apart. So we thought that it would be fun for us to switch places."

For quite a while after that news was delivered, neither girl said a word. Fritzi just stood there, looking quietly pleased with herself. Lulu also just stood there, angrily thinking about the things she didn't think.

Lulu didn't think being tricked was fun. She didn't think that losing five races was fun. And she certainly didn't think it was fun to be treated so—what was that word?—so condescendingly, like Fritzi was great and she was some pitiful thing. Just thinking about how not-fun it all was, Lulu got madder and madder. And if a parent hadn't been quietly lurking in the background, she'd have grabbed a huge hunk of Fritzi's hair and . . . pulled.

Instead, she made her meanest face and, in her meanest voice, she chanted this chant:

If I had met a wicked witch,
I'd happily have kissed her
If in exchange she swore
I'd never have you for a sister.

Fritzi, to Lulu's great annoyance, did not seem the slightest bit bothered by this chant, so Lulu decided to go for a second verse:

And if she'd wanted more,
Then ten more kisses I'd have
kissed her,
If ten times more she would
have sworn
You'd never be my sister.

Fritzi continued to barely pay attention. And this made Lulu so much madder than she'd been before that, even though a parent was quietly lurking in the background, she grabbed a huge hunk of Fritzi's hair . . . and pulled.

chapter nine

Very soon after, Lulu was once again sitting—with Fritzi—in Call-Me-Debbie's office. Being told (though she knew this already) that pulling someone's hair was unacceptable. Being told (though she doubted it) that what seemed like Fritzi acting condescendingly was Fritzi truly trying to be kind. Being told (though she disagreed) that anybody who had a good sense of humor would surely have thought the twin-switching trick was hilarious. And also being told that since she was the (temporary) older sister, she had to be better behaved than a younger sister, even when that pint-size (I won't bother with the other words) younger sister had beaten her at swimming and at Scrabble.

PLEASE RETURN TO FRITZI

Lulu, looking stormy and not sounding too sincere, told Call-Me-Debbie she'd try to be better behaved. And Call-Me-Debbie told Lulu that, because of this morning's Mitzi/Fritzi mix-up, she had decided—for the first time ever—to let Lulu's kid be exchanged for another kid. Now usually, at Camp Sisterhood, you're given a girl if your mom is having a girl, and you're given a boy if your mom is having a boy, and if your mom doesn't know what she is having . . . well, that's a whole other story I won't get into. However, because the only spare kid at Camp Sisterhood was a boy, Lulu—rather than getting a new younger sister—was going to get a new younger *brother* instead.

"Though it truly doesn't matter if it's a boy or if it's a girl," Call-Me-Debbie assured her. "A happy sister experience will always be a happy sister experience."

chapter ten

$\mathcal{B}\!\mathit{y}$ now it was time for another
yummy, delicious Camp Sisterhood lunch
(twelve to one), after which came an
afternoon (one to five) of freedom and
fun for the SITs who had spent the entire
morning (eight to twelve) trying to have a
happy sibling experience. Meanwhile, the
SITs who had spent the morning (eight
to twelve) having freedom and fun, now
got to spend the entire afternoon (one
to five) trying to have a happy sibling
experience.

(Are you following me? It isn't that
hard—keep up!)

The freedom and fun activities were—
just to mention a few—board games,
ball games, arts and crafts, swimming,
hiking, climbing, kayaking, computers,
and scavenger hunts. The happy sibling
activities were the same, except instead

of doing them with SITs who were more or less your own age, people that you chose and wanted to be with, you had to do them with some little kid who wasn't your first, or even your fiftieth, choice.

Which brings us to the next morning, when Lulu was introduced to Sebastian, whose older sister she was about to become.

(*Sebastian*—I've always liked that name except that it's one of those names that it's impossible to find a nickname for. *Seb? Sebbie? Bastie? Astie? Tinny? Yinny?* What? If anyone out there has a suggestion, please send a postcard to me. Meanwhile, Lulu is calling him Sebastian.)

Looking at Sebastian—with his bitten nails, untied sneakers, and runny nose—Lulu could tell that he was no Mitzi or Fritzi. He wouldn't be a talking machine. He wouldn't be condescending. He wouldn't be winning any kind of game. In fact, she was so positive that she would be beating him, all the time, at everything, that perhaps—as Sisterly Tip number two had suggested—she could even let him win every now and then. Though not a lot. Though maybe hardly at all. Though forget it—he should learn to be a good loser.

chapter eleven

Lulu's first few mornings being Sebastian's "older sister" proved how right she had been when she'd predicted that she would be beating him, all the time, at everything: running, swimming, shooting hoops, holding your breath underwater, plus any board game or card game you could think of.

Well, what did you expect? The kid was seven years and twenty-two days old! Except he didn't just lose—he was a disaster.

A disaster at one-against-one, and also team sports.

For instance, in all his volleyball games,
Lulu was constantly having to call a time-
out. Because he was constantly bleeding
and needing a Band-Aid. Because he was
constantly skinning both of his knees.
Because, though he constantly tied them,
he was constantly tripping over his untied
shoelaces.

He was also a disaster at most other
things.

If, for example, he hammered a nail
into one of those woodworking projects
he was working on, he hammered,
along with that nail, one of his thumbs.
And furthermore, he couldn't seem to
walk through a swinging door without
that swinging door smashing into his
face. And furthermore, when his work

assignment was helping to weed the Camp
Sisterhood vegetable garden, he pulled
out the plants and left in all the weeds.
And furthermore, each time he carried a
breakfast tray over to one of the dining-
hall tables, part of the breakfast would
always slip off the tray. And splash all
over his T-shirt. Then splatter all over the
floor. After which he would step in it.

The truth is (though it's not nice to say, and I'm sorry to have to say it), Sebastian was a clunky, clumsy, klutzy, also totally clueless, kid.

(Except, and this may astonish you, he wasn't! For later that summer, when camp and this story were over, a doctor figured out that Sebastian was having trouble seeing and needed *glasses*. And after he got his glasses, he wasn't clunky, clumsy, or klutzy anymore. And only just a *little* clueless—not totally.)

It would have made a good story, and it would have made Lulu a hero, if *she* had figured out about the glasses. But she didn't. Instead, though she wasn't majorly mean, she also wasn't what you'd call patient and kind. And yet, no matter how often she scolded and criticized Sebastian, no matter how often she told him, "Could you just, for once in your

life, try to watch where you're going!"
or "How many times can you make the
same mistake?" Sebastian kept saying
how lucky he was to have gotten Lulu for
his older sister. In fact (believe it or not,
and I find this practically impossible to
believe), Sebastian kept insisting that
Lulu was maybe the greatest person he'd
ever met.

(If a person who isn't your mom or your
dad keeps telling you you're the greatest,
it's not because, like moms and dads,
they *have* to. The reason they're probably
telling you this is because they really,
truly think you *are*.)

(Or maybe it's because they're totally
clueless.)

For all that Lulu had to do was announce, with absolute certainty, that Anchorage was the capital of Alaska to get Sebastian to say, with awe in his voice and awe in his eyes, "Amazing! Genius! Wow! You just know *everything*!"

(Well, not exactly everything—the capital of Alaska is actually Juneau.)

And if Lulu came to breakfast with her hair in a ponytail instead of straight down, Sebastian would swear she looked like a Disney princess.

(Well, Lulu looks perfectly fine but do me a favor and check out her picture. Now answer me—is *that* a Disney princess?)

And when Lulu told Sebastian some

silly joke, like, "Why did the chicken cross the road?" Sebastian would laugh till he almost wet his pants, after which he'd declare—and he really meant it—"That's the best joke I ever heard in my life!"

But Lulu never listened to Sebastian's

adoring words. She was way too busy criticizing and scolding him. She never heard his compliments because she was so sure that nothing he could say would be worth hearing. She tuned Sebastian out because she wanted to be finished with Camp Sisterhood, finished with its sibling-sweetness stuff, and finished with a kid so absolutely, totally clueless that he had to be told why that chicken crossed the road.

chapter eleven
and one half

(*Now* if, for some strange reason—like you're from another planet—you don't know why the chicken crossed the road, ask your mom or your dad to give you the answer. I personally think it's way too dumb to talk about.)

chapter twelve

 would, however, like to talk about Campfire Night at Camp Sisterhood. And Lulu would like to talk about it too. So she called up her mom and her dad on Saturday morning, the morning after Campfire Night, and happily announced, "I'm loving it here!"

"Loving it, did you say?" asked her mom.

"Here, as in Camp Sisterhood?" asked her dad.

"And," asked her mom, "just to check— is this Lulu we're speaking to?"

"Yes, it's me," said Lulu, sounding happier by the minute. "It's me, I'm here at Camp Sisterhood, and I love it."

"And why is that?" asked her dad, who was sounding a funny combination of pleased and confused.

"Because," said Lulu, "on Campfire Night they teach us how to be bad to our little sisters. Or, if we're getting a brother, our little brothers. They teach us how to do things that are definitely not nice—and it's so cool!"

"There must be some misunderstanding," said her dad.

"A terrible misunderstanding," said her mom. "We need to telephone Call-Me-Debbie immediately!"

So they did.

"What," asked Lulu's mom, "is this Campfire Night?"

"And what," asked Lulu's dad, "are you folks at Camp Sisterhood trying to teach our sweet little girl?"

"*Sweet* little girl?" said Call-Me-Debbie, but only to herself, and then she explained:

"On the first Friday night at Camp Sisterhood, there's always a Campfire Night, when all of the SITs sit around the campfire toasting marshmallows, while—one by one by one—each of the counselors take turns telling stories."

"Oooh," said Lulu's mom, "just like when I went to camp and everybody told ghost stories."

"Not exactly," Call-Me-Debbie replied. "These counselors are telling stories about the things that they did—things that they shouldn't have done—to their little brothers and sisters when they were young. Naughty and not-nice things. Bad and beastly things. Things that if I told you, you'd find shocking."

"So why in the world . . . ," gasped Lulu's mom, unable to go on.

". . . are you," continued Lulu's dad, "allowing them to tell these terrible stories?"

"Because," Call-Me-Debbie said proudly, "when they're finished with their stories, they tell the SITs how sad and sorry they are that they ever did such things, how ashamed and guilty they feel for having done them, and how very much they wish that they had treated their little sisters and brothers better."

"And then what happens?" Lulu's dad demanded.

"And then," Call-Me-Debbie replied, "all the SITs—well, *almost* all the SITs— understand how unhappy they'd feel and how awful it would be to engage in Bad and Beastly Big-Sister Behavior."

"*Almost* all the SITs?" Lulu's mom asked nervously.

"Almost, yes." Call-Me-Debbie sighed. "Because there's always somebody who listens to these stories and decides that she's hearing some Really Great Ideas."

"And could that somebody," Lulu's dad asked nervously, "possibly be a somebody that we know?"

"Possibly," was Call-Me-Debbie's not-too-comforting answer. "Let's wait and see."

chapter thirteen

We won't have to wait too long because now that Lulu has finished freaking out her parents, she's getting Sebastian and taking him on a hike. And she's thinking that on this hike she might try out some of that Bad and Beastly Big-Sister Behavior, which she so loved learning about last night.

For the truth is that Lulu didn't expect she'd be feeling one bit terrible if she did some not-nice things to a little sister. And although she wouldn't be beastly to a teeny-tiny new baby (who'd only know how to eat, sleep, cry, and poop), once that baby got big enough to get in her way and start messing with her stuff—watch out! There was plenty that a big sister could do to make a little sister very unhappy. And Lulu could practice doing it to Sebastian.

(Now why can't Lulu remember that she is up here at Camp Sisterhood to learn to *love* and *be nice to* her little sister? All I can say about this is that she should NEVER have been allowed to hear the wicked stories they told on Campfire Night.)

Sebastian, who was eagerly waiting to go on the hike with Lulu, tried, unsuccessfully, to give her a hug.

"Back off, Sebastian," said Lulu, "we're hiking, not hugging."

Sebastian backed off, slung his huge backpack onto his skinny back, then headed, huffing, up the mountain trail. Lulu, toting her backpack, walked behind him. And after some slow, sweaty hiking, she decided the time had come to try the BBBSBs she had learned from Counselors Veronica, Caitlyn, and Josie.

First try.

Lulu to Sebastian: "Everyone here at Camp Sisterhood likes me a whole lot better than they like you. Maybe you haven't noticed, but they do."

Sebastian—very cheerfully—to Lulu: "I've noticed that they do. And I do too!"

(Well, that didn't work.)

Second try.

Lulu to Sebastian: "I know this awesome secret, but I'm only going to tell you if you let me have all the candy your grandma keeps sending you."

Sebastian—very cheerfully—to Lulu: "Wow, an awesome secret! When will you tell me? Meanwhile, take the candy and also my flashlight."

(What is *wrong* with this kid?)

Lulu waited a little while and then she

made her third try, saying to Sebastian, with a sigh and deep disappointment in her voice, "I wish you were one of those kids who was strong enough to carry both backpacks—yours and mine. Too bad you're so little and skinny and wimpy and weak. Other kids your age can easily do it." (Not true! They can't!) "But I guess that they are all much stronger than you."

(Now this is how, Counselor Josie had confessed on Campfire Night, she had gotten her little sister to carry two great big bags of groceries up a steep hill. She didn't *make* her do it—her sister kept begging and begging Josie to let her do it, insisting, "Please, I'm strong enough! I'm strong enough! I am!" till Josie was finally forced—I mean, pretended to be forced—to say okay.)

So Sebastian, like Josie's sister, kept telling Lulu how strong he was until she finally allowed him to carry her backpack. And while, bent under his double load, he was huffing and puffing and huffing up the trail, Lulu—carrying nothing and quite pleased with how clever she was— was smoothly and unsweatily strolling behind him.

Until (and of course there had to be an until) Sebastian—crushed by the weight of both of those backpacks—stumbled, staggered, wobbled, pitched forward, and fell flat down, belly first, on the mountain trail.

There was silence, absolute silence, for a moment, and then Lulu asked, a little impatiently, "Talk to me, Sebastian. Are you dead?"

"No," Sebastian replied.

"Anything broken?" asked Lulu.

"No," Sebastian once again replied.

"So get up, and let's keep hiking," Lulu—who wasn't the most sympathetic of girls—told Sebastian.

Another long silence, and then Sebastian replied.

"I think I twisted my ankle when I fell. I think I'm done with hiking for the day." He turned his face so he could look deeply into Lulu's eyes, and maybe he was smiling and maybe he wasn't. "I think you'll have to carry me down the mountain."

Carry him down the mountain? *Carry him?* Carry him, and his heavy backpack, and also her heavy backpack, all the long way down that mountain trail? This certainly wasn't Lulu's idea of a wonderfully wicked BBBSB. But sweaty, smelly, dirty, achy, and unbelievably grumpy, Lulu wound up having to do it on this extremely hot Saturday morning near the end of her first happy week at Camp Sisterhood.

(Now some of you really smart readers are probably asking why Lulu didn't get any help from that parent lurking quietly in the background. *Surely you haven't forgotten that there was always a parent lurking in the background.* But that parent had decided that, since Lulu alone had gotten herself into this mess, Lulu alone would have to get herself out. What do you think? Is that fair? Is that right? I say yes!)

chapter fourteen

By the time they were down from the mountain—Sebastian slung over Lulu's shoulder, two backpacks hanging heavily on her back—Lulu was an exhausted wreck, and Sebastian's ankle was feeling much better. (Surprised?) Lulu, now finished with him for the day and having Sunday off, first took a long cool swim in the lake, then spent the rest of the weekend wondering why all her BBBSBs had failed.

Okay, so she'd gone too far when she tricked this skinny little kid into carrying two giant backpacks up a mountain.

And okay, he'd rather hear secrets than eat candy. And when she told him that everyone liked her better than they liked him, who knew he would say that *he* liked her better too? The things Lulu did to Sebastian didn't seem to make him unhappy. She needed to think a lot harder about what else she had heard on Campfire Night that would.

But dumping a mushy PB&J in her little brother's bed and pretending she put it there just in case he got hungry (Counselor Caroline's story) sounded too messy for Lulu to do to Sebastian, even though Caroline said that it was fun to watch her brother washing it out of his

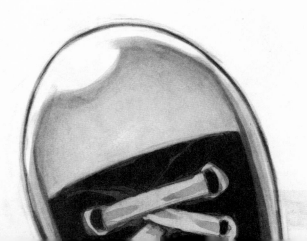

ears and nose and hair. And popping
out of a closet and screaming "boo" to
her little sister (Counselor Rosa's story)
sounded too lame for Lulu to do to
Sebastian, even though Rosa said that it
was fun to hear her sister's "Eeek! Eeek!
Eeek!" So maybe, Lulu was thinking,
she ought to forget about the stories
she'd heard on Campfire Night, and
chant Sebastian a bad and beastly chant
instead.

And so, on Monday morning, when Lulu
went to get Sebastian, she didn't say hello
or even wave. Instead, she looked him up
and down, frowned an unfriendly frown,
and started chanting:

I did not, and I do not, and
I'll never want a sibling
Whose shirt is smeared with
breakfast and whose nose is
always dribbling
And whose teeth are stuck
with pieces of the food that
he keeps nibbling
And who'll always and
forever be a nibbling,
dribbling sibling!

"You're such a good poet. That's such a good poem," Sebastian said to Lulu, completely ignoring the fact that he had been dissed.

For the hundredth time I'm thinking, What's *wrong* with this kid?

For there goes Sebastian—yet again—unbothered by Lulu's rude ways and telling her how wonderful she is. And there will go Lulu, not listening to what he is saying. Except this time, for reasons I don't understand and can't explain, Lulu is giving Sebastian her total attention!

"I AM a good poet. It IS a good poem," Lulu unshyly agreed, enjoying each one of Sebastian's admiring words. And though she had planned on chanting another bad and beastly verse—rhyming "sibling," "dribbling," and "nibbling" with "quibbling" (look it up)—she instead sort

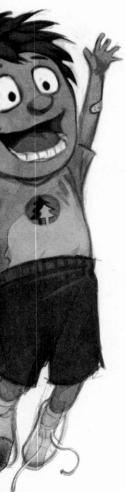

of smiled at Sebastian and told him, "Keep talking."

"And you're beautiful," said Sebastian, "and you tell the funniest jokes."

"And?" said Lulu, deciding she didn't need another verse. "Keep talking."

"And," Sebastian went on, "you know the names of all the state capitals and everything."

"True," said Lulu, not a bit bored with what Sebastian was saying. "You can keep talking."

To which Sebastian admiringly, adoringly replied, "And I'm thinking you're probably perfect— through and through!"

(Oh, cut it out, Sebastian! What are you *talking* about? Lulu's okay, but probably perfect? Please!) Yet Sebastian thinks she is, and Lulu really, really likes that he thinks she is. So perhaps it isn't surprising that Lulu is suddenly thinking a thought that she has somehow never thought before. She's thinking that having a younger sister might not be so bad—so hideous! so horrible! such a nightmare!—if that sister totally adored her.

And thought that she was a genius, a princess, a poet.

And did whatever Lulu told her to.

And gave Lulu all her candy, and also her flashlight.

And thought she was probably perfect—through and through.

Lulu is actually thinking that she might not mind at all having a little sister who believed that her big sister was maybe the greatest person she'd ever met.

In the time she had left at Camp Sisterhood, she was going to have to learn to teach a little sister to adore her.

chapter fifteen

(*Again* I'm asking why Lulu can't remember that she is up here at Camp Sisterhood to learn to *love* and *be nice to* her little sister. She isn't here to learn how she can teach her little sister to adore *her*. But that's what Lulu wants, and since Sebastian already adores her, she won't learn anything hanging around with *him*. So if she's going to figure out this adoration stuff, she must trade in Sebastian for another kid.)

On Monday, after lunch, Lulu announced to Call-Me-Debbie that she needed to exchange Sebastian for Mitzi. To which Call-Me-Debbie replied that there was a rule about not trading in your kid. To which Lulu pointed out that Call-Me-Debbie had already broken that rule. To which Call-Me-Debbie explained that breaking it once didn't make it okay to break it twice. To which Lulu loudly insisted, "But we won't be breaking it twice—we'll be *un*breaking it. We'll be putting things back the way they were before."

A long, long, long time later, Call-Me-Debbie, worn out from arguing with Lulu and desperately needing a cup of tea and a nap, finally told her, "Right. Okay. We'll compromise. I'm letting you trade in Sebastian. But in exchange you're taking both Mitzi *and* Fritzi."

Which was fine with Lulu.

"All right," said Lulu to Mitzi and Fritzi
when, the next morning, they gathered
in the vegetable garden. "Let's get
something understood right now. Mitzi,
you beat me at Scrabble. Fritzi, you
beat me at swimming. But you shouldn't
forget that I'm older and smarter and

better than you are at everything—
EVERYTHING—else."

"So?" Either-Fritzi-or-Mitzi said to Lulu.

"So," said Lulu, "here's how it should
go. I expect respect to begin with.
Followed a little bit later by admiration.
And a little bit after that, after you've

heard my jokes and rhymes and the names of state capitals, plus seen all the games and sports events I can win, you're going to decide that I'm probably perfect— through and through, and maybe the greatest person you ever met. After which you'll totally adore me."

Lulu, smiling proudly, was quite pleased with her presentation. The twins, however, weren't that impressed.

"We will?" said Either-Mitzi-or-Fritzi to Lulu. "I don't know about that."

"Especially since, I'm sorry to say"—and this must have been Fritzi speaking— "you couldn't beat me—not once!—in a swimming race."

"And never even heard of the word 'cacique'"—this was Mitzi speaking—"till I beat you at Scrabble."

"And furthermore," added Fritzi, "how many words—in five seconds—can you rhyme with it?"

"I told you I wasn't counting Scrabble or swimming," Lulu growled, "and furthermore," she continued, quick as a flash, "'beak,' 'cheek,' 'eek,' 'freak,' 'geek,' 'leak,' 'meek,' 'peak,' 'reek,' 'seek,' 'teak,' 'weak,' and 'Zeke.'"

"So how come you left out 'unique,' 'oblique,' and 'Mozambique'?" asked a most exasperating Mitzi.

"She did her very best," explained a most condescending Fritzi. "She probably doesn't know those fancy words."

"Let's start weeding this garden," hissed Lulu, who almost couldn't stop herself from doing or saying something she certainly shouldn't. "And I don't want

you pulling out anything but the weeds."

While they worked in the vegetable garden together, Lulu slowly calmed down, reminding herself that throwing a tantrum or yanking a hunk of hair wasn't the best way to get the girls to adore her. She decided, instead, to amuse them with her hilarious why-does-nobody-starve-in-the-desert joke. And after she finished asking them why, and after they both gave up, Lulu explained that nobody starves in the desert because of the SAND WHICH IS THERE!

After which there was not a whole lot of laughing. More like . . . none.

"Not the funniest joke that I ever heard in my entire life," said Mitzi.

"But not as bad," said Fritzi, "as that one about why-did-the-chicken-cross-the-road."

Lulu was starting to feel that this adoration thing might be harder than she'd expected.

"So," she said, changing the subject, "Bismarck. Carson City. Sacramento. Dover."

"What about them?" asked Either-Mitzi-or-Fritzi.

"They are the capital cities of North Dakota, Nevada, California, and Delaware," said Lulu, "and I know the other forty-six capitals too."

"Well, isn't she *maybe* the greatest!" said Mitzi to Fritzi.

"And *probably* perfect," said Fritzi, "through and through."

Lulu was getting angry again, angry like steam was coming out of her ears. So she chanted—but just to herself—a calm-down chant:

It doesn't matter if they
disrespect, mock, and ignore me.
Before this week is over, they will
totally adore me.

When Lulu had finished chanting, however, she was still feeling angry. So she chanted another verse of her calm-down chant:

It doesn't matter if they
are against instead of for me.
By Sunday morning both of them
will totally adore me.

Lulu was feeling less angry now, but still a little steamy, so she chanted one last verse of her calm-down chant:

*It doesn't even matter if they
out-and-out abhor me,
Because when I am done with them,
they'll totally adore me.*

There. Lulu felt calmer. Much, much calmer. (And I hope you're looking up the word "abhor.")

For the rest of her morning with Mitzi and Fritzi, she took them first for a quick dip in the lake and then to bookmark-making at arts and crafts, reciting state capitals all along the way. Some she got right and some she got wrong, but right or wrong, the twins were not impressed. Or amazed or astonished. And certainly not adoring.

"Ball games tomorrow!" Lulu
announced, determined to not be
discouraged. "Softball. Volleyball. And
some basketball too. I'll watch you play
and tell you everything you're doing
wrong. And then I'll get in there and show
you the right way to do it."

"Lucky us," said Mitzi, not sincerely.

"I'm sure you'll try," said Fritzi, too
sincerely.

And so, the entire next morning,
Lulu watched as Mitzi and Fritzi swung
at, swatted, and tried to sink the ball,

carefully pointing out to them what she
called their "many, many, many mistakes"
and then, in what only Lulu would think
was a kindly tone of voice, explaining
what they should do to, as she put it,
"maybe stop messing up all the time."
After which she got in there and showed
them what she herself described as "some
really good moves."

After which Mitzi and Fritzi had only one thing to say to Lulu: "It's time for lunch."

Where was respect? Where was admiration? And where, oh where, was even the teeniest, tiniest, slightest hint of adoration?

chapter sixteen

$\mathcal{Lulu}$ was not—repeat, NOT—a happy camper.

On Thursday she recited the names of all the US presidents, including a few that had never actually been president, and leaving out some that definitely belonged in. Still, of the forty-five she named, she did get thirty-one right, and the girls should have been impressed, except they weren't. Nor, when Lulu arranged her hair in some new, beguiling (that means very cute) hairdos, did either girl ever mention the words "Disney princess." And when she chanted a charming chant that rhymed "begins," "grins," "pins," and "fins" with "twins,"

1. george washington
2. abraham lincoln
3. john quincy jones
21. Ben Franklin
22. Bill
TOP Coif

the twins didn't even look up from what they were doing. And when she beat both Mitzi and Fritzi at several games of Bingo and suggested it might be time for them to admit she was probably perfect through and through, Mitzi answered, "How about Scrabble tomorrow?" and Fritzi answered, "And also a swimming race?"

And Lulu said, "Yes!"

Yes? Yes? She said yes? WHAT WAS SHE THINKING?

(I know what she was thinking, since I'm the person writing this story: She was thinking that maybe—no, certainly—the only thing that stopped those girls from adoring her was that they had beaten her at Scrabble and swimming. And so she was thinking that if, tomorrow, she could beat them both, they'd have no reason on earth to *not* adore her. And then she was thinking that if she really really really worked at it, she could beat them.)

So . . .

The rest of the day and all the way up until midnight, Lulu was nonstop studying Scrabble words. And then, from midnight till sunrise, since she couldn't practice racing in the lake, she practiced racing back and forth from her cabin through the dark woods to that far-off bathroom,

telling herself—and actually kind of believing it—that she was being chased by a girl-eating snake. Which made her run really really really fast. She also kept on telling herself (though this sounds kind of weird to me) that the faster she could run, the faster she'd swim.

On Friday after breakfast, Mitzi, Fritzi,
and Lulu headed for the games cabin,
where they found, to their astonishment,
that practically all of Camp Sisterhood was
already there. Word had gotten out that
Lulu and Mitzi were having the ULTIMATE
SCRABBLE CONTEST, and everyone wanted
to watch and cheer and boo and root for
the one they hoped would win.

Mitzi loved it!

She climbed up on a table and stamped her feet a few times till everyone paid attention, and then she started in with her, "So hello, and in case you don't know me, I'm Mitzi, I'm eight—well, practically eight—and I'm a twin, and—"

Lulu, impatient and irritated and determined to stop this talking machine from talking, lifted her up off the table, plunked her down on the floor, and firmly interrupted her for-sure-to-be-endless speech with "—and when we're done here, she'll tell you her favorite color and favorite song and favorite everything, but right now she and I are playing Scrabble."

And that's what they did, agreeing that the winner of two out of three would be the Official Scrabble Champion of Camp Sisterhood.

So . . .

Mitzi—no surprise here—won the first game. Then Lulu—who had memorized maybe a million billion new Scrabble words—won the second. But then—after playing slowly and carefully all the way through lunch—Mitzi and Lulu ended game three in . . . a tie.

That's right—I said tie.

Now, of course, there was only one thing to do—play another tie-breaking game. Except that when they did, they tied again. And then, of course, they needed to play another tie-breaking game. And so they did, and so they tied again. By now you're probably thinking that it's impossible to keep having tied games in Scrabble, impossible for Mitzi and Lulu to end three games in a row with the very same score. But in case that's what you're thinking, I would like to remind you once more that I—not you— am the person writing this story.

But though I'm writing this story, I was still surprised to hear, as a new game began, a voice from the rear of the room hollering, "Stop!" And then to see a skinny, messy, klutzy, clueless kid—Oh, no! It's Sebastian!—pushing his way to the front of the crowd and hoisting himself up onto the Scrabble table. And then to hear him saying in a firm, un-Sebastiany voice, "Both Mitzi and Lulu are winners. Both Mitzi and Lulu are champs. It's time to end the games so Mitzi and Lulu can share the victory by being named the Official Scrabble CO-Champions."

First there was silence. Then there was clapping. Then there was more clapping. And then Guess-Who was heard to indignantly say, "If we're going to share the victory by being named the Official Scrabble CO-Champions, you have to say Lulu and Mitzi, not Mitzi and Lulu."

chapter sixteen
and one half

In case you didn't notice, and though she didn't do it too nicely, Lulu has just agreed to SHARE with Mitzi.

chapter seventeen

After they'd finished their late, late lunch and rested their bellies a while, Lulu and Fritzi took themselves down to the lake. Again, almost all of Camp Sisterhood was there. And again, it was decided that the winner of two out of three (of the swimming races) would be the Official Swim-Race Champion of Camp Sisterhood.

But if you're guessing this contest, like the Mitzi-Lulu Scrabble games, wound up ending in tie after tie after tie, your guess would turn out to be absolutely wrong. For even though she had practiced all night, and swam as if a girl-eating snake was chasing her, Lulu was beaten by Fritzi—she was beaten BIG by Fritzi—twice in a row. Even though Lulu was taller, heavier, stronger, older, and fiercer, she had been beaten badder than she'd ever been beaten before by this pint-size, frizzy-haired, button-nosed, blue-eyed, and unbelievably speedy not-yet-eight-year-old.

I repeat—Fritzi didn't just beat her—

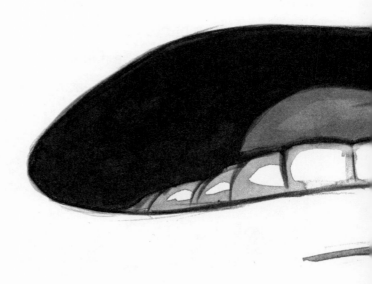

she beat her BIG, she beat her BAD, she REALLY BEAT HER.

"You were amazing," said Call-Me-Debbie to Fritzi.

"Amazing," said Mitzi.

"Amazing," Sebastian said too.

And then—because it suddenly seemed impossible not to say it—Lulu grumpily, grudgingly said to Fritzi, "I guess I have to admit that you were amazing."

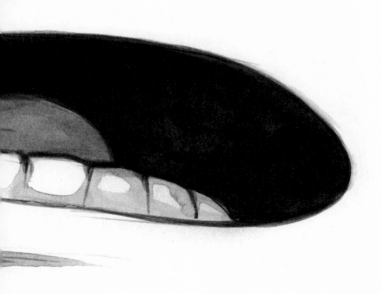

chapter seventeen
and one half

In case you didn't notice, and though she didn't say it too nicely, Lulu has just said Fritzi was amazing.

chapter eighteen

That Friday evening a second Campfire Night was held at Camp Sisterhood. But this time no one told their wicked tales. Instead, while all the counselors and little brothers and sisters listened, Call-Me-Debbie asked each of the sisters-in-training to talk about what she had learned while she was there. And she beamed a blissful smile as SIT after SIT told how she had discovered the joys of sisterhood.

And then it was Lulu's turn.

She said that she had learned some Bad and Beastly Big-Sister Behavior.

She'd learned some beguiling ways to fix her hair.

She'd learned that sharing was actually better than losing, although she'd always much rather WIN than share.

She'd learned a million billion cool new Scrabble words.

She'd learned that saying to someone, "You were amazing," wasn't as horribly

hard as she thought it would be.

She'd learned that no matter how really, really badly she needed to go, she still could make herself wait until morning to pee.

She'd learned that veggie burgers and cucumber salad and slimy stewed fruit wouldn't kill her or even make her sick.

She'd also learned that if she could pick between getting a little sister and getting a tooth pulled, she still wasn't sure which one she would pick.

And another thing: She had learned
that when people decide they don't adore
you, there's nothing you can do to make
them adore you.

Call-Me-Debbie, not so blissful,
just had this to say: "Would
anybody like to make a
comment?"

They would.

Mitzi said to Lulu, "I don't adore you. But I do respect and admire you for learning all those cool new Scrabble words."

Fritzi said to Lulu, "I don't adore you. But I do respect and admire you for being able to tell me I was amazing."

Sebastian said to Lulu, "I respect you, I admire you, and also I adore you—but what do *I* know?

chapter nineteen

On Saturday morning, their final morning together, Lulu took Mitzi and Fritzi for a hike. Each of them carried only her own heavy backpack. There wasn't much conversation—not even from Mitzi, the talking machine—for they all were too busy huffing and puffing and sweating. And even though Lulu was deeply tempted to name the names of the planets, in order, out loud, she just said, "Mercury, Venus—" and then she stopped.

Saturday afternoon, Lulu hung out with the other SITs. And then, as Call-Me-Debbie had promised on the very first day, it was time for that great big end-of-camp celebration, time for everybody at Camp Brotherhood to join with everybody at Camp Sisterhood for fun and games and a yummy, delicious meal.

(In case you've already forgotten about this end-of-camp celebration, you'd better go back and reread chapter four.)

And yes, there was fun, there were games, there was what some folks might call a yummy, delicious meal. There were also many speeches and many prizes, including a Swim-Race Champion ribbon for Fritzi, and two Scrabble CO-Champion ribbons for Mitzi and Lulu (whoops, excuse me, LULU and Mitzi).

There was also a lot of mingling among the SITs and the BITs and their "siblings."

Which is how the trouble began.

A group from both of the camps started taking turns—one by one—shooting basketballs into the baskets. Lulu and Sebastian were part of the group.

Sebastian was his usual untied-shoelaces, breakfast-all-over-his-T-shirt self, and was scoring his usual—zero—basketball score. And after his fifteenth miss, a Camp Brotherhood BIT began laughing and pointing at him and saying, in between ha-ha-ha's, "Hey, kid, you must be doing this on purpose. No one can miss the basket *that* many times." After which he poked Sebastian's food-smeared T-shirt, and said, "But I guess you miss getting stuff in your mouth a lot too."

This time, I swear, there really was steam coming out of Lulu's ears. She leaped in the air! She roared a ferocious roar! And then she was standing between Sebastian and the BIT—her eyes kind of popping, her face turning redder than

red—clutching the BIT's shirt collar in her fist.

"You don't get to talk to Sebastian that way—ever ever ever. Take it back and tell him you're sorry," she said. "He's a messy kid and a klutzy kid but mainly he's *my* little kid, and the only one who can pick on him is . . . me!"

The bigger boy mumbled "sorry," wriggled out of Lulu's grip, and darted away as quickly as he could. Sebastian stood frozen in place, open-mouthed with amazement. Then Lulu tossed the ball to him and growled, "Okay, now shoot! And try to remember it's *basketball*, not *bowling*."

(So what's going on with Lulu? She just SAID what's going on, but I'll tell you again. Sebastian belongs to HER. He is HER little sibling. She protects him the way she protects all her other stuff. Which means she won't let anybody criticize him, or embarrass him, or laugh at him. Anybody, that is, except herself.)

Okay, I hope you've got it, because you'll be seeing her do this again—right after Mitzi and Fritzi trick a bunch of brothers-in-training into thinking that they, the twins, are only one person.

Which they just did.

After the twins were done with their trick, the BITs were annoyed, then extremely annoyed, and then INFURIATED. For Mitzi started dancing her triumphant victory dance and shouting, "We fooled you. We fooled you. We fooled you. We fooled you." And then Fritzi smiled her pitying smile and whispered (quite unsoftly) to her sister, "We probably fooled them because they're not too smart."

At this, the BITs howled with anger and

yelled some unfriendly words at Mitzi
and Fritzi, words like "gloaters" and
"show-offs" and "smarty-pantses," and
more words like "sneaky" and "rude" and
"condescending," and then some more
words that I can't mention here.

To which our Lulu responded by doing
her red-faced, steam-coming-out-of-her-
ears thing again. After which she warned
the boys in her best make-them-shiver
voice, "They're little. You're big. So leave
them alone, you bullies. Say one more
word, and I'll make you sorry you did!"

Then grabbing each girl by an arm, she
marched them away.

Both of the girls thanked Lulu for sticking up for them.

"Those boys were fools," said Mitzi.

"Those boys were such fools," said Fritzi.

"Those boys *were* fools," said Lulu, "BUT YOU WERE TOO! That twin trick! That victory dancing! That gloating! That saying they weren't too smart! All that's stuff you're not supposed to do!"

"So how come you stuck up for us?" asked Mitzi.

"So why, if we're fools," Fritzi asked, "were you on our side?"

"Because even though you can certainly sometimes be fools," Lulu replied, "you are *my* fools. Because," she continued, half-irritated and half–something else, "sisters have to be on their sisters' side."

chapter nineteen and one half

I'm letting you figure out what that "half–something else" is.

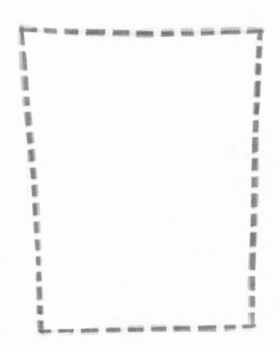

chapter twenty

$\mathcal{A}fter$ the end of the end-of-camp celebration, and after an early Sunday morning meal, the SITs' parents came to take their girls home.

Lulu astonished her mom and her dad by thanking Call-Me-Debbie for what she carefully told her was "a sort-of, kind-of, maybe, not-exactly-wondrous, life-expanding experience."

She astonished them again by giving Sebastian, Mitzi, and Fritzi good-bye hugs. (Not HUGE hugs. Just LITTLE hugs. But still . . .)

And then she climbed into the car and astonished her mom and her dad once again by saying, as they headed back toward home, "I've been thinking, and what I'm thinking is that getting a little sister might not be as bad as getting a tooth pulled."

The End

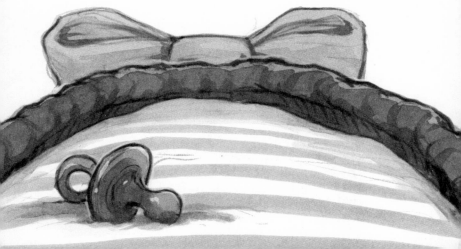

The

End

(Really.)